Cutielocs
And the Three Stylish Bears

Written by
April Bush

MYND MATTERS

To purchase books in bulk or for additional information, contact Mynd Matters Publishing
715 Peachtree Street NE
Suites 100 & 200
Atlanta, GA 30308
www.myndmatterspublishing.com

ISBN: 978-1-957092-58-4 (pbk)
ISBN: 978-1-957092-59-1 (hdcv)

Illustrator: Derreck Washington

FIRST EDITION

To my daughter Caylee, my nieces Jordan, Marlei, Ivy, Kenedi, and all the little girls in the world. Always read and believe in yourself.
Find great friends that will help you grow!

To my sisters, Angel and Ashley, two of the most stylish in our crew. Thanks for your support!

Once upon a time, on a sunny afternoon in southwest Georgia,
lived a smart and beautiful little girl named Cutielocs.
She was very fashionable and sweet as can be.
She was looking forward to the Daddy-Daughter Dance later that night.
The only thing on her mind was to make sure her outfit was just right.

A couple of blocks down the street,
in a beautiful two-story log cabin,
lived three stylish bears.

Big sister bear loved jewelry. Middle sister bear loved shoes.
Baby sister bear had a style of her own,
which always included glitter of some kind.

The three stylish bears woke up from a nap and went down for lunch. Big sister bear had ordered pizza, but it was sizzling hot and needed time to cool off.

So they decided to go for a walk down the street to the local shop.

Cutielocs needed a few more things to make her outfit just right.
So, on to the local shop she went.

As she walked down the street, a nice cabin caught her eye. Cutielocs walked up to the cabin and found the door slightly ajar.

She walked in and a familiar aroma drifted her way. "I am kind of hungry and love pizza," said Cutielocs.

She tried the first slice of pizza.
"Oh my, this slice has way too much meat."
Then, she tasted the second slice of pizza.
"Oh no, this slice has no meat at all."

Finally, she gobbled down the third slice of pizza.

"Oh my, I love pepperoni pizza, and this is just right!" she exclaimed.

"Now I'm a little tired, I think I need a nap."

Cutielocs headed upstairs.
She looked inside the first room
and was shocked.

16

"Earrings, yes! I need some bling!"
Cutielocs thought the first pair of earrings were way too long.
The second pair of earrings were much too short. As Cutielocs
took off the earrings, she dropped the back and could not find it.
She excitedly picked up the last pair and said, "These are just right!"

Cutielocs walked into the room. "OMG! Look at all those purses!"
On the wall were shelves of purses in so many colors, shapes,
and sizes. They were big, small, bright, dull, and even sparkly.
Cutielocs picked up the first purse. "Oh no, this purse is way too big."

She looked on another shelf. "This purse is too dull,"
she said, somewhat disappointed.
Then she looked at another purse and smiled. "This purse is just right!"
She put on the purse and walked out of the room.

On her way to find a bed, Cutielocs walked past the closet, and she just had to see what was in there. "Shoes!" she shouted.
She tried on one pair of shoes.
"Oh my, these are too high," she laughed.
Then she tried on another pair but said,
"Oh no, these are too low."
She then saw a shiny pair in the corner.
"These are just right!"

Cutielocs put on the sparkly shoes and walked out of the closet
and over to the big mirror. She remembered seeing a radio
on the dresser and decided to play some party music.
As she danced in the mirror and all around the room,
Cutielocs did not hear the three stylish bears return home.

As the three bears walked into the kitchen,
Big sister bear said, "Hey! Someone took a big bite out of my pizza"
with attitude. Middle sister bear said angrily, "Someone took a bite out
of my pizza too!" Baby sister bear crossed her arms and poked out her
lips. "My pizza is gone, so somebody has gobbled it all up."

The three sisters heard music coming from upstairs.
They ran up the stairs and into the first room.
Big sister bear said, "Hold up! Someone has been messing
with my earrings." Middle sister bear looked around and said,
"Someone has been messing with my earrings too,
and the back is missing." Baby bear's eyes got watery,
and she shouted, "My favorite earrings are gone!"

The sisters ran to the next room.
"Has someone been in here?" asked big sister bear.
"Someone has moved my purse," said middle sister bear.
"Someone has moved my purse," baby sister bear said.
"Wait! The music is coming from the back room," yelled big sister bear.

Walking past the closet, big sister bear looked inside.
"Someone has moved my shoes," she said.
Middle sister looked in the closet and said,
"Someone has moved my shoes too." Baby sister bear was shocked.
"Someone has taken my shoes, and I see who has them on!"
As Cutielocs took a selfie, she saw the three bears in the background.
She immediately turned around and yelled, "I love your style!"

Without waiting for a reply, Cutielocs asked, "Please, can I buy these items from you? Tonight is a very special night, the daddy–daughter dance, and these accessories are just right!" The sisters had a quick meeting and agreed to sell her the accessories. Cutielocs was overjoyed!

Cutielocs had everything she needed for her outfit. She rushed back home to get dressed. Everything was perfect. As they prepared to leave the house, her dad said, "You are so beautiful! Are you ready to dance?" Cutielocs replied, "Yes, this is the best day ever!"

DADDY daughter Dance $

The sister bears decided to open their own shop and name it, The Beary Cutie Fashion Boutique. Cutielocs visits the shop almost every week to talk and pick up something cute and chic from her new bear friends.

Beary Cutie Boutique

27

CPSIA information can be obtained
at www.ICGtesting.com
Printed in the USA
BVHW011459100323
660175BV00008B/568

9 781957 092591